Edouard de Pomiane

# Cooking in Ten Minutes

*faber and faber*

LONDON · BOSTON

First published in 1948
by Bruno Cassirer, Oxford
First published in this edition in 1967
by Faber and Faber Limited
3 Queen Square London WC1N 3AU
Reprinted in 1968, 1970 and 1976
Reissued in 1985

Printed in Great Britain by
Whitstable Litho Limited
Whitstable, Kent
All rights reserved

English translation © Bruno Cassirer, Oxford, 1948

*British Library Cataloguing in Publication Data*

Pomiane, Edouard de
Cooking in ten minutes
1. Cookery
RN: Edouard Pozerski   I. Title
II. Benton, Peggie
641.5     TX717
ISBN 0-571-13599-4

## PREFACE

I AM neither a fool nor a micromaniac (which is the opposite to a megalomaniac and means a man with a passion for exiguity. This word, by the way, is not to be found in the dictionary). And yet the day my book " Cooking in Six Lessons " appeared I was called frivolous. I was criticised for teaching the art of cooking in six lessons when everyone knows it takes ten years to become a cook. I replied to this criticism in a preface showing the part that science can play in the rhythm and measure of teaching any art, including cookery. I tried to show that I had a feeling for speed and that I didn't simply disregard the question of time.

Now I maintain that one can prepare a meal in ten minutes, and as this is an incredibly short time I shall be treated as a micromaniac.

I shall not try to explain or defend myself. I shall try to convince you by describing all the dishes that can be prepared in ten minutes, only, of course, in towns where the necessary materials can be obtained. If you have to catch your fish in a limpid stream before preparing it then you will need more than ten minutes, even if you devour it raw, sprinkled with salt.

My book is meant for the student, for the *midinette,* for the clerk, for the artist, for lazy people, poets, men of action, dreamers and scientists, for everyone who has only an hour for lunch or dinner and yet wants half an hour of peace to watch the smoke of a cigarette whilst they sip a cup of coffee which has not even time to get cold.

Modern life spoils so much that is pleasant. Let us see that it does not make us spoil our steak or our omelette. Ten minutes are sufficient—one minute more and all would be lost.

First of all I must tell you that this is a lovely book, because I have only got as far as the first page. I have just sat down to write. I am happy, with the happiness of beginning a fresh task.

My fountain pen is full of ink; I have fresh sheets of paper before me. I love my book because I am writing it for you. I feel that I need only let my pen run on and I shall make myself clear. And my ideas move more quickly still.

My book will only be ten pages long. . . . It will seem absurd . . . and above all, incomprehensible.

As deliberation is in the very nature of science, I shall turn to it for calm and tell you everything you ought to know before beginning ten-minute cooking, even if you only want to boil an egg, which is done in two and a half minutes.

The moment you come into the kitchen light the gas.  Ten-minute cookery is impossible without gas.

Put a large saucepan of water on to the fire. Slip on the lid and let it boil.

What is the use of this water, you will ask? I don't know. But it is bound to be useful, either for cooking or washing up or making coffee.

If you are going to fry something don't wait to take off your hat before putting the pan on the fire. The time during which the fat melts and reaches the proper temperature does not count in the preparation of our meal.

The fire is busy. Now turn your attention to cooking.

There are four different ways of using heat for cooking: 1. Boiling, or cooking in water. 2. Cooking in fat or frying. 3. Cooking on an open flame (grilling). 4. Steaming.

In our case, that is to say when time is short, steaming is almost out of the question. It is a long, slow business and best avoided by people in a hurry.

We will keep to the first three ways of cooking.


## BOILING

If you want to cook quickly by this method, begin by plunging the food into boiling salted water. Now this is waiting on the fire.

As time is limited you can, of course, only boil small pieces of food. In spite of this, it is possible, as you will presently see, to boil a slice of leg of mutton weighing a pound. This is a dish for two people blessed with a good appetite. You can also cook a piece of beef of the same weight tied round with string. This is a most worthy dish.

Do not try to cook vegetables. It is impossible in such a short time. You can, however, prepare

FRYING

If boiling means cooking in a liquid at a temperature of almost 212°, deep frying means cooking in a liquid at a temperature of almost 392°.

One must therefore first of all heat the fat to a maximum. You will know that the temperature is right when smoke rises from the surface. At this moment put in the food, otherwise the fat decomposes and yields substances which damage the meat, or whatever you are frying, and the food is spoilt.

Contact with the food lowers the temperature of the fat and the situation is saved. You have used the fat at its maximum temperature.

Remember that you can only fry food in small pieces. Potatoes should be sliced and only small fish attempted.

The food which is to be fried must be perfectly dry. Otherwise the moisture evaporates suddenly on coming into contact with the boiling fat. This phenomenon is accompanied by spluttering fat and water. Be careful of your clothes; see that the fat does not catch on fire. This is not dangerous, however. Just cover the pan with a cloth or a lid and the danger is averted.

If the food in question is difficult to dry—fish, for example, which is naturally covered with moisture—dip it in flour. This makes it dry and fit for frying.

Put the food into the smoking fat. Leave it there for about five minutes. Then lift it out. Let the fire blaze until the fat begins to smoke once more. Plunge the food in again. Wait two minutes. Lift it out and drain. Sprinkle with salt, and then eat it scorching hot.


GRILLING

You can produce an excellent grill on a gas stove. You need only brush the meat lightly with a feather dipped in oil or melted butter before exposing it to the heat.

How should one grill? It is simple. Just rely on your own common sense.

In order to be a success, a grilled cutlet should be brown outside and rosy with all the juices of the meat inside.

In order to keep the juice in the meat one must prevent it from escaping. For this purpose one must harden the surface and create an impenetrable envelope. Nothing is simpler. The meat contains albumen. Albumen coagulates and hardens under the action of heat. Since you wish to achieve sudden hardening and a rapid coagulation you must expose the meat at once to a very high temperature.

If you wish to grill something, turn on the grill before you take off your hat while you put the pan

minutes, either on a spit, in the oven or in a fireproof dish.

However, if you have a slice of meat you can roast it in a frying pan.

You will often make use of this method in ten-minute cookery. It is a bastard technique related to both frying and roasting.

You can cook meat, fish, vegetables, fruit, eggs and some sweets in a frying pan. This technique is worth our consideration.

COOKING IN A FRYING PAN

Everything we have said about frying and about grilling applies to cooking in a frying pan.

If you put butter or fat in a frying pan, do not begin to cook your food until the fat is smoking. Let the fat be very hot from the moment the food comes into contact with it and start straight away with a blazing fire. In order to avoid unpleasant smells, open the kitchen window.

Turn the food as soon as one side is golden brown. Once both sides are browned cooking can continue on a gentler fire, so lower the flame. Salt. When you lift the meat from the pan a reddish deposit is left sticking to the bottom. It is formed partly of coagulated albumen but chiefly of caramel derived from the sugar in the meat. Cooks call this " *glace*."

Pour some liquid into the pan. This boils, dissolves the *glace* and you have a delicious sauce.

You can prepare a considerable number of sauces by dissolving the *glace* in your frying pan in different liquids. I only suggest the following: water, white wine, port or madeira, brandy, beer, meat broth, red wine, etc. What treats await you!

## THICKENING WITH FLOUR

If you like smooth sauces thicken them, that is to say, lend them a velvety quality which they do not of themselves possess. You can achieve this by adding a little flour to the liquid.

In order to obtain an agreeable result one must follow certain rules which are based, actually, on common sense.

Starch binds sauces because on coming into contact with water and under the influence of heat it thickens. If you throw the flour abruptly into the sauce only the outside turns to starch. Instead of obtaining a smooth sauce you will achieve only a few lumps of cooked flour swimming in a watery liquid. The sauce is spoilt.

In order to make a smooth sauce and avoid the disagreeable flavour of flour proceed like this:

Put a small piece of butter into the frying pan with the *glace*. Add a teaspoonful of flour. Mix

boil. The sauce is finished.

## THICKENING WITH EGG

One can thicken a sauce or a soup by adding one or more yolks of egg. Here one must be still more careful. The yolk of an egg thickens when it is heated in a liquid to about 144°. Above this temperature it hardens and coagulates and the liquid curdles.

Only add the egg to the luke warm liquid. Put it on a moderate fire, stirring all the time. Dip your finger in the liquid from time to time. When the heat becomes intolerable reduce the fire, keep on stirring and wait for it to thicken. Do not try to make the mixture too thick. You risk disaster. The liquid will certainly thicken as it cools.

These are the fundamental rules for cooking in ten minutes. It is the very least that everyone must know. To the reader who wishes for further information I recommend one of my books on gastronomics*.

---

* "Bien manger pour bien vivre" (Albin-Michel, Paris).
"Le Code de la bonne chére" (Albin-Michel, Paris).
"La Cuisine en six lecons" (Editions Paul-Martial, Paris).

# SOME ADVICE

## AND

# THE KITCHEN EQUIPMENT

In order to cook it is not necessary to possess a large number of utensils. You can hide all your equipment in a small cupboard and take it out as you want it.

You will need:

A set of aluminium saucepans ranging in diameter from five to nine inches with a lid for the largest one only.

A small grey enamel saucepan of four and a half inches diameter.

Two iron frying pans with absolutely flat bottoms, measuring seven and eight inches across.

A pan for eggs.

A small kettle holding a pint and a half.

A colander.

A pan for deep frying with a draining basket.

A funnel.

A ladle.

A skimmer.

A wire frying slice.

A wire whisk.

A large kitchen knife.

An ordinary knife.

Kitchen spoons and forks.

of the two frying pans. The deep frying pan will need a good deal of space, it is true, but this is the only bulky object. If you use oil for frying pour this, when it has cooled, into a can, using a funnel.

Ladle, knives, spoons, forks, whisk and wooden spoons can be kept in a drawer.

All you have to do now is to decorate the kitchen with some gastronomically stimulating pictures hermetically sealed under glass to protect them from the inevitable steam and particles of fat.

Gas, as we have already said, will be your indispensable ally; but if you want to take full advantage of all it can do for you, see that the burners of your stove are clean.

How should one clean them when they are greasy?

Nothing simpler: lift out the movable parts and brush them in soda water. Before putting them back make sure that no hole is stopped up.

See that the fumes of the stove are carried off through a ventilator.

Open the window as often as possible.

Wash the enamelled walls of your kitchen once a week with luke warm soapy water.

Your kitchen will thus be a spotlessly clean laboratory which you will transform, I am sure, into an artist's studio.

MENUS

FOR

LUNCH

Poached eggs with black butter
Fried fillets of veal
Green peas
Salad with cream dressing
Cheese
Fruit

21

Cold sausage with olives
Mutton chops
Sauté potatoes
Salad
Cheese
Chococlate éclairs


Escargots de Bourgogne
Quails à la Crapaudine
Asparagus with oil and vinegar
Cheese
Fruit


Noodles à la Tchèque
Entrecôte with onions
Cucumbers and cream
Cheese
Fruit salad


Boiled haddock
Escalopes of veal Zingara
Salad
Cream cheese
Fruit


Hot shrimps
Fried chipolata sausages
Purée of green peas
Cheese
Fruit

Tripes à la Mode de Caen
Green peas with ham
Salad
Cream cheese with pineapple

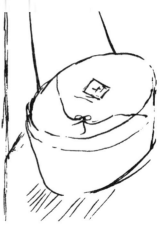

Scrambled egg with truffles
Venison cutlets
Chestnut purée
Salad
Cheese
Fruit

Skate with black butter
Beans à la crème
Potato salad
Cheese
Fruit


Mussels with saffron
Spinach
Tomato salad
Omelette flambée
Fruit

# SOME MENUS FOR DINNER

Potage au jambon

Escalopes viennoise
Haricot beans à la crème
Salad
Cheese
Fruit


Pea soup
Cutlets Pojarski
Beetroot salad
Cheese
Fruit salad


Semolina soup
Calf's head tortue
Salad
Omelette flambée
Cheese
Fruit

Onion soup
Hare à la crème
Beetroot
Salad
Cheese
Puits d'amour


Broth with beetroot
Pigeon en casserole
Sauté beans
Cheese
Cœur à la crème


Greek Soup
Cold chicken with mayonnaise
Tomatoes à la Polonaise
Cheese
Chestnut cream


Estragon soup
Sauté chicken with mushrooms
Salad
Cheese
Cream buns


Mushroom soup
Frankfurter sausages
Potato salad
Cheese
Cœur à la crème

Pumpkin soup
Cod à la crème
Green peas
Cheese
Fruit

Fruit

Lobsters à l'Americaine
Tournedos Rossini
Asparagus with oil and vinegar
Cheese
Fruit

# SOME ADVICE REGARDING BEHAVIOUR
## AT TABLE

I do not pretend to pose as a professor of etiquette. You know how to behave at table, naturally. But my own experience with meals when one is host, entertainer, cook, parlour maid, carver and butler all at once entitles me to offer you some practical advice.

You have just glanced at some pages of menus which can be quickly prepared. They consist of several dishes, each of which only takes ten minutes to prepare. To make three dishes, therefore, you would need half an hour unless you divide your time skilfully between them.

Remember that you can prepare two dishes at once on the two burners which your gas stove must, as a minimum, possess. The third dish should, if possible, only need warming up. This can be done on a low gas while you are eating the first two dishes. Always arrange your menus so that the third dish can cook itself. For example, do not attempt sauté potatoes, but warm up green peas or sauerkraut.

If you wish your hospitality to be charming, *reduce your journeys to the kitchen to a minimum.* Make your preparations with foresight. Have a small table within reach for clean plates, cheese and dessert.

Put used plates on to this table.

Each time you go to the kitchen (and you must

never go more than twice) take as many plates with you as possible so that the table is clear for dessert.

Never let your guest help. This brings an atmosphere of chaos and destroys the repose which

Fruit
Coffee

Would you prepare the different dishes one after another in the order in which they are given? No, for you would be courting disaster.

When you come home:

1. Put the large saucepan of water on the gas. Cover it. (This is an invariable rite.)

2. Open the tin of peas. Empty it into a bowl. Put it on one side.

3. Beat the eggs in a second bowl, salt and add grated cheese.

4. Put the lettuce leaves, washed, into a salad bowl. Add oil, vinegar, salt and pepper, without mixing. Stand on one side.

5. Grind the coffee and put it into the coffee machine. Put on one side.

6. Heat some butter in a frying pan until it smokes, brown the fillet first on one side and then

the other. Eight minutes are sufficient. Add the peas, draining off the water first. Leave it on a low fire.

7. Move the saucepan of water to one side. Heat some butter in a frying pan until it smokes. Pour in the eggs and make the omelette; three minutes.

Sit down to table.

Eat the omelette while the peas are warming.

The fillet reaches perfection and reclines, golden brown, on a jade green carpet.    Put the pan of water back on the fire.

Stir the salad and eat it.

A slice of Brie with a curl of butter will delight you.

Before skinning your orange pour two cups of boiling water on the coffee which is massed in the filter of the machine. It will draw out all the aroma while you are eating the fruit.

Everything is finished . . . no, it is only just beginning. Put the coffee pot back on the gas for twenty seconds.  Watch it like a lynx.  Whatever happens the coffee must not boil.

Warm a cup by rinsing it out with boiling water. Fill it with hot coffee. Sink into your comfortable armchair; put your feet on a chair. Light a cigarette—Turkish or Virginian, according to your particular weakness. Send a puff of smoke slowly up to the ceiling. Sniff up the perfume of your coffee. Close your eyes. Dream of the second puff, of the second sip. You are fortunate.

At the same time your gramophone is singing very softly a tango or a rhumba.

Of course, if there are two of you, you will need two fillets of veal, two cups of coffee and two cigarettes. But ten minutes are sufficient for preparing the main dish.

appear first on the table, so do not lose any time.

# HORS D'ŒUVRE WITHOUT
VARIATIONS

Do not rush into complicated *hors d'œuvre*. You have not the right, nor the time. In any case they only attenuate the voluptuousness of your hunger for the principal dish, so use them with parsimony.

If you have a passion for *hors d'œuvre*, have the courage of your convictions and make a whole meal of these gastronomic frivolities.

This will reduce your cooking to the infinitely simple, that is to say, to the preparation of coffee.

Bring home some mortadella or salami, some tunny fish, some olives, mushroom salad and three slices of smoked ham. Add some butter, a slice of Roquefort cheese, some fruit, and you will be happy.

But be careful. Do not repeat this *dînette* often. It would damage your health. And in any case you will soon get tired of it.

You can, however, perfectly well begin your meal with one of the delicacies mentioned. Do not make an egg dish on that day. You will eat your tunny fish or your two sardines while the pork chop which will afterwards appear with chestnut purée is turning a crisp golden brown.

Do not eat sardine unless there are two of you as, however small it may be, a tin of sardines is very large for you alone. You should not keep preserved food from one day to the next once it has been taken out of the tin in which it

delightful surprise.

A stick of crisp white celery, dipped in mustard is a delightful *hors d'œuvre*.

Black olives and some smoked sprats bring visions of the east, especially if you precede them, in summer, with a small glass of *schnaps* and a large glass of fresh water.

Black caviare is reserved for millionaires and they are not interested in ten-minute cookery. For you and me there is only pink caviare. An ounce or two of this does not cost more than a box of sardines. Eat it on slices of bread and butter. Sprinkle it with a few drops of lemon juice.

A single slice of raw smoked ham is not ruinous. If it is perfectly tender it should melt in your mouth. Follow it with a mouthful of buttered bread.

Experiment with a thin slice of raw bacon. Sprinkle it with the lightest dusting of paprika.

No one—except perhaps your doctor—can forbid you to start your meal with half a dozen

Portugese oysters, which you will bring home already opened. Accompany them with a slice of black bread thickly buttered, a glass of very dry white wine and half a lemon.

Sometimes the oysters can provide the whole meal. You must then serve them *à la bordelaise*. On those days buy a dozen oysters. Crisp some chipolata sausages in the frying pan. Eat a burning sausage, then allow your mouth the cool caress of an oyster. Repeat this twelve times . . . and then a cup of coffee. That is all.

Avoid salads as *hors d'œuvre*. It is too cheap. One eats too much because one is hungry at the beginning of a meal—and repents it five minutes later.

I have already said too much about *hors d'œuvre* because my object was only to prescribe them in homœopathic doses.

If I have not convinced you, do as you like. It is, after all, the best way of being satisfied with what you eat.

# ULTRA RAPID SOUPS

Can one prepare a soup in ten minutes? Certainly, if one is content to keep to a few rules. Boiling a saucepan of water is the slowest part of the business. The time this takes does not count according to our agreement, as we begun our culinary manœuvre by putting a saucepan of water on the gas.

Here are twenty odd soups, all of which can be rapidly prepared.

## BOUILLON

I do not pretend to show you how to prepare broth from meat in ten minutes, but there are pastes, cubes and extracts on the markets which, when dissolved in water, produce a distinct flavour of meat broth.

Some preparations are horrible. They are not derived from meat, but are the result of chemical action on blood serum. They are bad preparations. They are very cheap but of no gastronomic value.

On the other hand, there are preparations

Add a teaspoonful of liquid meat extract. Let it boil for a few minutes in order to dissolve the extract completely. Salt. Add a tiny piece of butter. Let it melt. Serve in two teacups.

## SEMOLINA SOUP

Prepare some bouillon according to the above directions. As it boils pour slowly two spoonfuls of very fine semolina into the saucepan, stirring as you pour. As soon as the soup boils once more lower the gas and let it boil from seven to ten minutes. It is ready. Serve it in two soup plates.

## POTAGE AU JAMBON

Prepare some semolina soup. While it boils cut a slice of ham into tiny pieces. When about to serve the soup sprinkle in the rosy fragments. Let it boil once only. Serve.

## GREEK SOUP

Prepare some semolina soup. When it is finished, lift it from the fire. Break an egg and drop the yolk into a bowl. Mix it with a spoonful of hot soup. Then add a second and a third spoonful. Pour the contents of the bowl into the saucepan which is still standing away from the fire. Mix it carefully. Add the juice of quarter of a lemon. Serve immediately before the soup has time to cool.

## POTAGE VELOUTE

Prepare three-quarters of a pint of bouillon. Let it boil. Mix a spoonful of potato flour with a little cold water. Pour this into the boiling broth, stirring all the time. Boil on a low fire for five minutes. Draw the saucepan from the fire.

Put two yolks of egg into a small soup tureen. Stir them with two spoonfuls of hot bouillon. Add a third and a fourth spoonful, then pour in the whole of the soup, stirring continuously. The soup is ready.

## POTAGE VELOUTE WITH TARRAGON

Prepare some velouté soup as above. At the moment of serving add some tarragon leaves.

## BOUILLON WITH PARMESAN

Prepare some bouillon. Serve, adding in the soup plate, some grated parmesan and fragments of toasted bread.

## BEETROOT SOUP

Prepare three-quarters of a pint of bouillon. Let it boil.

Take a quarter of a pound of beetroot, which has been cooked in the

has a wonderful crimson tint.

You can serve this soup in two different ways: as it is, or thickened with two ounces of double cream just at the moment of serving.


## CREME DE CEPES*

Prepare three-quarters of a pint of bouillon. While it is boiling mix a dessertspoonful of barley flour with a little cold water. Pour it into the soup, stirring all the time. Put an ounce of dried mushrooms into the saucepan. Let them boil for a good ten minutes, or better still, if you will forgive me, a quarter of an hour.

Put the soup through a sieve. Remove the mushrooms. Add three ounces of double cream. It is ready.

* Cèpes are a kind of mushroom not usually gathered, but you can obtain them dried, in packets, at most large stores.

## ONION SOUP

Cut a large onion into small pieces. Melt some butter in a frying pan and heat it until it smokes. Add the onions. Make a hot fire so that they brown quickly. Let them turn the colour of mahogany.

Add a small teaspoonful of flour and stir well. Mix the *roux* with some tepid water. Make it up to three-quarters of a pint by adding hot water. Pour it into a saucepan. Put in on the fire. Let it boil for eight minutes. Salt. Pepper. Pour the soup on to slices of bread sprinkled with grated parmesan. Serve.

You can add a little warm milk, some cream or a beaten egg to the soup.

## SORREL SOUP

Melt a piece of butter in a saucepan. Add two ounces of sorrel, carefully washed. Stir it over the fire. The sorrel turns into a sort of paste. Add three-quarters of a pint of boiling water.

Scatter two soupspoonfuls of semolina into the soup, stirring all the time. Let it boil six minutes. Salt. Add two ounces of thick cream. Serve.

## TOMATO SOUP

Boil three-quarters of a pint of water in a saucepan and stir in a good soupspoonful of tomato extract.

Add two dessertspoonfuls of fine semolina, stirring as you do so. Salt. Let it boil six minutes. Add two ounces of thick cream. Serve.

## PUMPKIN SOUP

Take half a pound of pumpkin. Peel it and cut the pulp in pieces the size of a nut. Put them in a saucepan. Cover with boiling water. Let it boil six to eight minutes. Crush the pieces. Salt

saucepan. Add a bay leaf, a spoonful of olive oil and then three-quarters of a pint of hot water. Salt. Pepper. Let it boil from eight to ten minutes. Take the saucepan off the fire. Put two yolks of egg into your soup tureen. Add half a ladle of your garlic broth. Mix it well. Pour in the rest of the broth, stirring all the time. Add four slices of stale bread. Serve.

If there are two of you, consume this fragrant soup in unison, otherwise the one who refrained would find it hard to bear the other's proximity during the evening.


## PEA SOUP

You can, of course, only prepare this soup from flour. You cannot dream of using the dried vegetables when time is so short.

Remember that vegetable flours do not easily turn into starch. The result is that when the soup is made it is not creamy. The flour sinks to the bottom and the water swims on top. In order to avoid this, always add a little wheat flour. This forms starch and the vegetable flour remains suspended.

To Prepare Pea Soup:

Take a saucepan and put a lump of butter into it. Melt it. Add: 1. a teaspoonful of flour, 2. two dessertspoonfuls of green pea flour; mix it all over the fire. Add, little by little, stirring all the time, three-quarters of a pint of tepid water. Salt. Let it boil six minutes. Serve with little pieces of toast.

POTAGE ESAU

Proceed as above using lentil flour instead of pea flour.

FISH SOUP

Buy the head of a small cod or similar fish. Cut it into eight pieces. Buy half a pound of whiting and clean it. Put the fish into a saucepan. Cover with a pint of boiling water. Add salt, pepper, a bay leaf, a pinch of powdered saffron and a spoonful of olive oil.

While it is boiling mix two tablespoonfuls of rice flour with a little cold water. Pour it into the boiling liquid, stirring as you do so. Let it boil ten minutes. Put six slices of stale bread into a soup tureen. Pour the soup through a coarse sieve into the tureen and crush the fish with a pestle. Serve the tureen containing the slices of bread soaked in this delicious soup.

44

# EXTEMPORARY SAUCES

Do not imagine that ten-minute cooking is going to condemn you to an eternal round of beef-steak without any of the frills of finer cookery.

Your gas stove has two burners, if not three. What is to prevent you cooking slices of ox kidney sauté in butter on the one, while you make a *sauce béarnaise* on the other?

During the same ten minutes you can prepare both the kidneys and the sauce.   The result is delicious. I have done it time and again. Thanks to the sauce the ordinary ox kidneys, despised by the fastidious, assume an aristocratic manner.

You can always prepare meat and a sauce, but are there many rapidly prepared ~~~~ ? Th~~~

## WHITE SAUCE

This is a horrible sauce, but at least it can be improved according to your taste. Then it becomes enjoyable. On principle, white sauce is simply starch paste buttered and salted.

This is how it is prepared: Take a small saucepan and a little wire egg whisk. Put a piece of butter the size of a large walnut and a small dessertspoonful of flour into the saucepan. Put it on the fire. The butter melts; use the egg whisk to whip the butter and flour into a smooth paste. Stir, little by little, a glass of cold water into the mixture.

The liquid thickens under the influence of the heat. Smooth out the lumps as they form. Let the sauce boil up. Add salt. Lift it off the fire. Add a little piece of fresh butter. The sauce is ready. It is not a good sauce, let us admit it frankly. So never use it as it stands. Ennoble it. Transform it into the sauces which follow.

## SAUCE NORMANDE

Prepare a white sauce as I have explained to you. Draw it off the fire. Add two ounces or so of thick cream. Stir the whole thing well. Put it back on the fire. Let the sauce boil up once. It is ready.

What should you serve this sauce with? With boiled fish, for example.

## SAUCE SUPREME

Prepare a *sauce normande*. Add a little liquid meat extract, sold in a bottle. You strengthen the sauce and completely change its flavour.

This sauce is a marvellous accompaniment to white fish, fried veal cutlet or any white meat.

## SAUCE AURORE

Prepare a *sauce normande*. Add at the last moment a trace of tomato purée so as to tinge the sauce with coral. Serve boiled mussels covered with this sauce. You will receive many compliments.

## SAUCE POULETTE

Make a white sauce. When it has only just left the fire beat in two yolks of egg. Add a trace of liquid meat extract, too.

## BECHAMEL SAUCE

This is a white sauce considerably improved by the fact that you moisten the mixture of butter and flour with cold milk instead of water.

Proceed like this:
Take a piece of butter the size of a large walnut

and melt it in a saucepan. Add a small spoonful of flour. Mix well. Then gradually, stirring all the time, add the cold milk. The mixture thickens. Stop adding milk when the sauce, while boiling, has reached the desired consistency. You will need

Let it boil, stirring all the time. Lift it off the fire; the sauce is ready. Serve it with hot boiled vegetables. You can obtain excellent tinned vegetables everywhere; they need only be warmed up. This is very convenient—an inestimable aid.

CURRY SAUCE

There are as many different kinds of curry as there are Hindoo cooks. Each one brings back from the spice market the different components of the curry and measures and mixes them himself. The curry powders on the market usually represent a good average.

To prepare a curry sauce in the French manner make, first of all, a Béchamel sauce; add according to your taste more or less curry powder. For the above quantity of sauce you will need at least half a teaspoonful of curry powder. Mix carefully. Boil for a second. Serve with hard or soft boiled eggs.

## SAUCE PIQUANTE

Up till now we have only considered white sauces. Brown sauces are also based on butter and flour, but this is longer on the fire before it is moistened. As a result, it turns brown. This is what cooks call making a *roux*.

The *roux* can be made more rapidly if one browns a few pieces of onion in the butter before adding the flour.

*Sauce piquante* is a brown sauce. Prepare it like this:

Put a frying pan on the fire. Melt a piece of butter and heat it until smoking. Add half an onion chopped fine. Increase the fire, stirring the onion round in the butter. It colours rapidly, becomes golden, then red, then mahogany brown. At this moment add a spoonful of flour; mix well. Wait till the flour browns a little. Stir in little by little a glass of water. Let it boil. Add a teaspoonful of vinegar. Boil again. Add three gherkins cut in slices. Finally, a little liquid meat extract. This is a perfect sauce. It is the classic accompaniment to pork cutlets fried in another saucepan on another fire.

## MUSTARD SAUCE

Make a sauce piquante, but instead of gherkins add a good teaspoonful of mustard. Classic accompaniment to fried herrings.

## SAUCE ROBERT

Prepare a mustard sauce. Add, at the last moment a spoonful of tomato purée. Excellent with veal and pork.

Nothing simpler than preparing a mayonnaise.

Take a fresh egg and a bottle of oil. Both should be at the same temperature as the room, but not a chilly room, of course. If the oil is too cold, if it is partly coagulated, you are courting disaster. Break the egg and put the yolk into a bowl. Get someone to pour the oil. You yourself armed with a wire beater or a special mayonnaise mixer, or even simply with a fork, stir the mixture of oil and yolk of egg. Your partner must pour the oil very slowly, drop by drop at the beginning, and then in a thin trickle. Mayonnaise is quickly made. Add salt and a drop of vinegar. Serve it with fish or cold meat.

## SAUCE HOLLANDAISE

The technique of a *sauce hollandaise* is considered difficult even by experienced cooks. In reality, nothing is easier. If you desire success, do as I tell you. You will certainly succeed.

51

Put a spoonful of cold water, a little salt and two yolks of eggs into a small saucepan. Put this little saucepan into a large one containing boiling water holding the smaller one firmly. Stir quickly, with a fork, the mixture of water and yolk of egg. This begins to thicken. At this moment lift the small saucepan out of the water, add two ounces of butter cut into pieces the size of a nut. Put it back into the hot water. Stir the mixture all the time with a wire beater. The butter melts and the sauce becomes creamy. Lift it out of the water a little. Add two more ounces of butter cut in pieces. Stir. Put it back into the water. The sauce thickens. Keep on stirring. Dip your finger into the sauce. If it burns, lift the saucepan out of the hot water. Stir fifteen seconds more. The sauce is ready. It should be thinner than mayonnaise. It should, however, coat a spoon which you dip in and lift out again. If you like the flavour of lemon, add a few drops at the beginning of the operation, before the butter. You are then much more likely to be successful with your sauce.

I have never succeeded in spoiling a *sauce hollandaise*. Follow my example.

This sauce is a luxurious accompaniment to boiled fish or tinned asparagus warmed in its own juice.


## SAUCE BEARNAISE

*Sauce Béarnaise* is *sauce hollandaise* perfumed with vinegar and shallots.

Peel a shallot and cut it very fine. Put it into a saucepan with two spoonfuls of vinegar. Put it on the gas. Boil it until the vinegar has evaporated considerably. Add a spoonful of cold water. Salt. Lift it off the fire. Add two yolks of ...

... p ...

some butter in a small saucepan. Add a soupspoonful of tomato and mix well. Add little by little some hot water, stirring all the time so that the tomato liquefies. Stop as soon as the sauce pleases you. Salt.

# SOME INSTANTANEOUS EGG DISHES

## BOILED EGGS

Nothing is easier than boiling two eggs. Your saucepan of water is bubbling on the gas. You place in turn two large fresh eggs on a spoon and lower them carefully into the saucepan. If there is enough water it will start to boil again immediately. Wait two and a half minutes, lift out the eggs, put them into egg cups and without waiting a second slice off the tops and eat them with crisp bread, fresh butter, the finest sauce and a glass of cool, dry white wine. This is a feast.

## SOFT EGGS

Put the two fresh eggs into the saucepan of boiling water. Wait five minutes. Take them out and plunge them into cold water. Wait ten seconds. Shell them carefully without damaging the whites. Put the eggs on a plate and pour melted butter, *sauce Mornay* or tomato sauce over them.

# Menu

## HARD BOILED EGGS

Proceed as before but leave the eggs ten minutes in boiling water. Take them out; plunge them into cold water. Wait till they have cooled.

Serve them as they are with salt, butter and mustard. They are better still with grated horse-radish, lightly vinegared.

Hard boiled eggs harmonise with all the cold sauces: mayonnaise, vinaigrette, tomato.

## POACHED EGGS

Nothing is simpler than poaching eggs. Take a middle-sized saucepan half-full of boiling water. It is standing on the gas. Break a very fresh egg into a tea cup. When the water boils, tip the cup, close to the surface, so that the egg slips in. The white sets immediately. The egg assumes a fairly regular oblong shape. Let it boil for a good minute. Lift it out with a skimmer. Let it drain. Put it on a plate, trimming off the irregular scraps of white. Prepare the second egg in the same way. Pour over them melted butter, butter browned over the fire, any white sauce, or a brown sauce flavoured with a little burgundy.

## FRIED EGGS

Heat some oil to smoking point in the deep frying pan. When the oil is very hot, that is to say when it is smoking merrily, drop in an egg which you have broken into a tea cup.

Immediately the egg puffs up and forms immense bubbles, which you burst with a fork. Wait thirty or forty seconds.

Lift the egg out of the pan, using a skimmer. Put it on to a warm plate. Salt. Fry the second egg immediately after the first.

This is a delightful accompaniment to some chipolata sausages which you have already fried for six or seven minutes in butter.

## OEUFS SUR LE PLAT

Take a fireproof dish and put it on the gas. Melt a walnut of butter and as soon as this is ready break two eggs and slide them gently on to the butter. The white sets immediately. B...

## EGGS AND BACON

Take two very thin slices of bacon. Melt some butter in the fireproof dish. Lower the gas. Lay the two slices of bacon on the butter, each cut in two so as to cover the bottom of the dish. When the fat is transparent break two eggs into the dish. Turn up the gas. Proceed as above. Salt very lightly. Pepper with discretion. Put the dish on to a plate. Eat slowly, sprinkling the dish, if you enjoy experiments, with your favourite brand of sauce.

## EGGS AND HAM

Buy a slice of York ham. Proceed as above but substitute ham for the bacon.

## EGGS WITH CERVELAT SAUSAGE

Buy a cervelat sausage. Skin it. Cut it in slices a quarter of an inch thick. Proceed as for " eggs and bacon," replacing the bacon by three slices of cervelat.

Half your sausage is left over. Eat it as *hors d'œuvre*, cut in cubes and seasoned with oil, vinegar and mustard.

## EGGS WITH CREAM

Heat some butter in a fireproof dish. Break in two fresh eggs. Proceed as if you were making *oeufs sur le plat*. When they are half-done add a teaspoonful of thick cream. Spread it all over the free surface of the dish. It liquefies. Salt and dust with paprika. Eat this dish with a glass of white wine well chilled.

## SCRAMBLED EGGS

You will need two eggs. It is difficult to scramble a solitary egg as it sets too quickly.

Break two eggs into a bowl. Beat them with a fork. Salt.

Melt and heat a large walnut of butter in a frying pan. Pour in the eggs and as soon as they begin to stick to the bottom of the pan break them loose with the back of the fork, stir them, worry them, torment them, mix them, beat them, so that all the lumps are broken up. Stir them on a gentle fire. When the eggs begin to thicken draw them off the fire. Stir. They continue to set. As soon as the eggs are ready, that is to say still creamy, pour them on to a slightly warmed plate. Eat immediately.

You can add all sorts of things to scrambled eggs as variations before you begin to cook them:

Cervelat cut in cubes.
Minced ham.
Tinned green peas

small quantities. Eggs with green peas must not become green peas with eggs.

One must receive, above all, the impression of creamy eggs cooked to a turn. The flavour of the addition must be of secondary importance. Besides, scrambled eggs with green peas are a delightful spectacle, while green peas with eggs are a depressing sight.

## OMELETTE

Nothing simpler than making a successful omelette. It is enough to have a frying pan which doesn't stick, that is to say, quite flat and not ballooning at the centre.

Break two eggs into a bowl. Beat them. Salt them.

Put the pan on to the gas. Melt a large piece of butter. As soon as it is smoking pour in your eggs. They thicken on coming into contact with the heat.

61

Now shake the frying pan continuously to prevent the omelette from sticking. With the help of a fork lift the edges of the omelette, tilting the pan so that the liquid egg is engulfed beneath the solid.

Shake the pan all the time. When you judge that there is only enough liquid to make the omelette creamy at the centre, take a porcelain dish. Tilt the frying pan. Let the omelette slip until it touches the dish. At this moment turn the pan as if you wanted to cover the dish.

This gesture rolls the omelette over itself and it is lying in the dish. Serve immediately.

One of the secrets of success is not to use too many eggs in a small pan. So never try to make an omelette out of six eggs in a pan which only holds two or three.

An omelette, like scrambled eggs, can have all sorts of additions. Repeat those which we have mentioned in connection with scrambled eggs.

# SOME OF THE FEW KINDS OF " PATE "

## WHICH CAN BE PREPARED

IN LESS THAN TEN MINUTES

" Pâte " covers all farinaceous dishes such as noodles, macaroni, spaghetti, dumplings, etc.

Remember that in England these are always cooked too long and served as a shapeless mass. This is why they are not particularly popular.

On the other hand, you can neither cook spaghetti nor macaroni in ten minutes. Only noodles can be prepared so quickly.

So let us cook some noodles. In order to prevent them sticking you must cook them in plenty of boiling salted water. This is the moment when you will bless the large saucepan of water which you put on the fire on reaching home.

As soon as the noodles are submerged turn up the gas. The water begins to boil once more. Be careful, it will boil over. Lower the flame and wait. In eight to ten minutes the noodles are cooked. You know this because they are no longer crisp when you bite them. Now you can prepare them in many different ways.

## NOUILLES A L'ANGLAISE

As soon as the noodles are cooked, empty the saucepan into a colander. Drain. Put them back into the hot saucepan. Add a large piece of fresh butter. Let it melt. Stir. Serve.

## NOUILLES A LA TCHEQUE

Prepare some *nouilles à l'anglaise*. Add some finely minced ham. Serve without cheese.

## NOUILLES A L'ESPAGNOLE

Prepare some *nouilles à l'anglaise*. Add some boiled mussels.

## NOODLES WITH GRAVY

Boil some noodles in salted water. Prepare two fried fillets of veal on another fire. At the moment of serving take out the fillets, dissolve the glace in the pan with a little hot water and turn the drained noodles into this gravy. Serve the noodles with the fillets.

## ALSATIAN DUMPLINGS

Beat an egg in a bowl with half a glass of cold milk. Little by little add some flour, beating with a whisk, until you have a very light semi-fluid paste. Smooth out the inevitable lumps.

In the meantime you have put a saucepan of salted water on the gas. It is boiling.

Using a teaspoon, scoop up some paste and plunge it into the water. Knock the spoon sharply on the edge of the saucepan. The ball of paste drops into the water.

Be quick and use all the paste to make at least fifteen little balls, which are as many dumplings. Let them boil five minutes without boiling over. Tip them into a colander. Put the dumplings into the saucepan without any water. Add some fresh butter and let it melt. Serve.

You can vary the additions and the flavouring and you will achieve as many different dishes: tomato sauce, gravy, melted salt pork, thick cream, butter and grated cheese, etc.

## RAVIOLI

In Italian shops in Soho one can buy ready made *ravioli*. All you have to do is to boil them. Cook them for eight to ten minutes in boiling salted water. Drain. Pour tomato sauce over them and sprinkle with grated parmesan. Serve.

# FISH WHICH ONLY ASK TO JUMP

# FROM THE FRYING PAN

In ten minutes you have just time to boil a small fish. You have plenty of time to cook it in a frying pan, and still more time to fry it in fat.

You see that your only difficulty will be in making a choice when you decide to replace meat by fish for your main course.

## WHITING

Boil some salted water in a saucepan. Add a spoonful of vinegar, a bay leaf and some spices—pepper, mace, curry, etc.

Take the fish which has been cleaned by the fishmonger and carefully washed by you, and plunge it into the saucepan. Let it boil ten minutes. During this time melt some butter and squeeze in a few drops of lemon juice.

Lift the fish out of the water carefully so as not to damage it.

Put it on a dish, sprinkling with melted butter and breadcrumbs.

## SKATE WITH BLACK BUTTER

Boil a pound of skate for ten minutes in salted, vinegared water.

In the meantime melt two ounces of butter in a frying pan. Add some chopped parsley. The parsley browns—the butter too. It turns the colour of mahogany. Lift the pan from the fire. After a few minutes add a teaspoonful of vinegar. (It does not splutter too much as the butter has already cooled a little. Otherwise the hot butter would spurt out of the pan on coming into contact with the vinegar.) Lift the skate out of the water. Drain it. Put it on a dish. Pour the black butter over it. Pepper a little. Salt to your taste. Serve.

## HADDOCK

Plunge half a pound of haddock, previously washed, into a saucepan of boiling unsalted water. Let it cook for ten minutes. Lift it out of the water. Drain. Serve with melted butter and lemon juice.

## COD WITH TOMATO SAUCE

Plunge one or two slices of cod rather less than an inch thick into a boiling saucepan of spiced, salted water. Let them boil ten minutes and serve with tomato sauce.

Salmon or any other large fish may be used for this recipe.

## HALIBUT SAUCE MORNAY

Plunge a piece of halibut weighing half a pound in a saucepan of boiling, spiced salt water. Let it cook for ten minutes. Drain. Serve with *sauce Mornay.*

Any fish can be cooked in salted water in ten minutes as long as it is cut in thinnish slices. Vary your sauces and you will have a number of different dishes.

## FRIED HERRING

Heat some oil to smoking point in a frying pan. Take a cleaned herring, dry it and roll it in flour. Put it into the pan. Lower the gas and open the window . . . the smell is penetrating. Brown one side of the fish for five minutes. Turn it. Five minutes more and it is ready. Salt. Serve as it is or with mustard sauce . . . This is a classic.

## FRIED MACKEREL

Wash the mackerel, which has been cleaned by the fishmonger, and dry it carefully. Make little cuts here and there on both sides. Dip it in flour.

which you have just bought under cold running water, as they are always covered with salt. Wash them and cut through the base of the heads. Pull the heads off and the intestines will follow. Dry the fish. Fry them, without dipping them in flour, in a pan containing smoking oil or very hot butter. Do not salt.

Serve with curls of butter and half a lemon.

## TRUITE MEUNIERE

This is a luxurious dish. But actually the satisfaction it gives you is not worth the expense of buying these precious fish in town.

Town trout are " artificial." They are born in an aquarium and fed too scientifically. They are flabby and have no resemblance to trout from a stream. Treat them like herrings, that is to say, clean them, wash them, dry them, flour them and cook them in a frying pan in butter which is very hot indeed, but not brown. Salt. Serve with the butter in which they are cooked adding even a little more.

## BOILED TROUT

You must buy live trout. Put a little saucepan containing a teacupful of vinegar on the gas. Let it boil. Put the receptacle in which you are going to cook the trout, filled with salt spiced water, on the gas.

In the meantime, kill the trout by striking their heads on the edge of the table. Clean them. Wash them. Put them into a hollow dish. Pour the boiling water over them. They turn azure blue. Plunge them straight into the boiling salted water. Cook them seven to eight minutes. Lift them out of the water. Drain. Serve with melted butter.

## FILLETS OF SOLE WITH MUSHROOMS

Buy some ready prepared fillets of sole. Buy at the same time half a pound of mushrooms.

When you reach home cut off the sandy base of the mushroom stems. Wash them in plenty of water, and throw this away together with the sand it contains. Begin again. Do not peel them, it is a waste of time—and mushroom. Cut them in slices. Wash them once more, lift them out of the water. Dry them. Put a frying pan on the gas with a piece of butter the size of a large nut. When it is smoking, put in your four fillets of sole. Warm for a minute. Turn. Cook for a moment. Add the mushrooms.

Make a very hot fire. The mushrooms ooze water.
Salt. Pepper. Add half a wineglass of dry white
wine. Let it boil hard. The water evaporates. The
ten minutes are over. Lower the fire. Add a piece
of butter mixed with a little fl

Wash the cleaned plaice. Dry it. Flour it. Fry
it in a pan containing smoking butter. Salt. A slice
of lemon.

## FRIED WHITEBAIT

When you reach home put the deep frying pan
on the gas. Clean the whiting and dry them. Dip
them in flour. Throw them into the smoking fat.
Wait five minutes. Take them out. Heat the fat for
three minutes. Plunge in the fish for two minutes.
Take them out and drain them. Salt. Slices of
lemon.

## FRIED WHITING

Only use small whiting; otherwise your ten
minutes will not be sufficient. Wash two small
whiting which have been cleaned, dry them and
flour them. Fry them in the same way as whitebait.

## FILLETS OF COD VIENNOISE

Have some slices of cod cut from the tail end. Let them be thin—say, half an inch.

While the basin of fat is heating put out three plates. One contains flour, the second a beaten egg, and the third breadcrumbs.

Dip the fillets of fish: 1. into the flour, 2. into the egg, and 3. into the breadcrumbs. Throw them into the smoking fat. Let them cook eight minutes. They are ready. Salt. Garnish them with slices of lemon and two sprigs of parsley which have been dipped into the hot fat for twenty seconds.

## BOILED COD

Buy some tinned fillets of salt cod. This is very economical and keeps a long time. You dip into this tin as parsimoniously as you wish. One fillet is enough for you alone. Take it, and keep the tin in a dry place for another time.

During the night before you eat the cod, soak the fillet in cold water. Change the water two or three times. Put the fillet into boiling unsalted water. Let it cook from five to six minutes. Take it out of the water. Drain. Put it on a dish, pouring melted butter over it. Decorate with a slice of lemon. Serve. Drink a glass of very dry white wine. Or rather two, because cod, so they say, is thirsty for butter and makes those who eat him thirsty too.

## CREAMED COD

Prepare a *sauce normande* while the cod is cooking. Mix fish and sauce. Savour it.

## BISCAY COD

Boil the cod. Prepare a tomato sauce, replacing the butter by olive oil. Add a green pimento cut in thin strips. Let it cook five to six minutes. Serve the cod with the

Put the deep frying pan on the gas. Let the oil smoke. Dip thin strips of salt-free fillet of cod in flour. Fry from eight to ten minutes in very hot oil. Serve with sprigs of parsley which have been dropped into the boiling oil.

# MOLLUSCS

The number of molluscs which can be prepared rapidly is relatively limited. They are, however, not to be despised as they constitute exciting and very nourishing dishes.

First of all oysters, which one brings home ready opened. Sprinkle them with some drops of lemon juice. Eat them with slices of brown bread generously buttered. Wash them down with white wine well chilled.

## OYSTERS AND SAUSAGES

Fry some chipolata sausages. Serve them very hot on a dish and on a second dish a dozen oysters.

Alternate the sensations. Burn your mouth with a crackling sausage. Sooth your burns with a cool oyster. Continue until all the sausages and oysters have disappeared.

White wine, of course.

## SNAILS

Buy a dozen snails from a concientious tradesman, that.is to say, a man who will use good butter for stuffing his snails.

Arrange the twelve snails on a large fireproof dish. It is not as easy as it sounds. The opening of the shell must face upwards. Otherwise as soon as the butter melts it runs out of the shell and the snail becomes dry and tough.

When you have arranged the shells properly, pour a little water into the dish. Put the dish on the fire for three to four minutes, just long enough to warm it. Then put it under the grill. In five to six minutes the butter has melted and the snails are hot. Eat them as long as they burn your fingers.

## MOULES MARINIERE

Buy two pounds of mussels. Wash them in running water, making sure that each shell is full. In order to discover this try to slide the two halves of the shell across each other. If the mussel is empty the two halves slip and the shell opens. All that remains to be done is to throw it away. It contains mud and impurities and might have spoilt your whole dish.

When the mussels are washed put them in a saucepan. Cover. Put them on the gas. In five minutes the shells are open. The water they contained is now boiling and the mussels are cooked.

Add a little pepper, some very finely chopped parsley and two ounces of butter, which melts in the salt water. This dish is as exquisite as it is simple.

## MOULES POULETTE

If you want to cook in the grand manner, arrange the cooked mussels in a deep dish. Pour the water into a small saucepan. Add some butter and warm it up; draw it off the fire and thicken with one or two yolks of egg. Be careful not to let it boil. Serve this sauce in a sauceboat.

## MUSSELS WITH SAFFRON

Cook two pounds of mussels. Put them on one side. Warm their water with an ounce of butter and a little saffron. Thicken with 100 grammes of thick cream mixed with a teaspoonful of flour. Serve the mussels with the sauce separately in a sauceboat. This is a feast.

# SHELLFISH

It is sometimes possible to buy live shrimps. Buy half a pound; wash them in fresh water while a small saucepan of water is coming to the boil.

Salt the water copiously. When the water boils throw in the shrimps, taking care that they do not jump out of the saucepan. Boil five minutes. Serve very hot with slices of fresh bread and butter.


## DUBLIN BAY PRAWNS A L'AMERICAINE

Heat a spoonful of olive oil in a saucepan. Add a good spoonful of concentrated tomato purée. Salt slightly. Stir in a glass of white wine; half a glass of madeira. Plunge half a pound of Dublin Bay prawns into this sauce. Season with paprika or a suspicion of cayenne pepper. Cover. Let them cook eight minutes. Add a small glass of champagne. Cook for five minutes. Salt to taste. Sprinkle with parsley. You will enjoy this dish.

## LOBSTER WITH MAYONNAISE

Buy half a cooked lobster. Serve it with mayonnaise. Use the few moments which you will still have left to decorate your dish with some lettuce leaves, green or black olives, capers, etc. You will feel yourself becoming an artist.

# SOME VEGETABLE AND OTHER

## ACCOMPANIMENTS

I want to consider vegetables before meat dishes. This, it will be said, is contrary to habit and tradition. But remember that we are upsetting tradition by producing a finished dish of vegetables in ten minutes when it is essential to cook vegetables for half an hour before beginning to prepare them.

So this chapter will be very brief because it will be reduced to the vegetables which can be cooked in a few minutes, to vegetable flour which can be bought ready prepared, to tinned vegetables and those which can be bought ready cooked.

The preparations which follow are principally accompaniments for meat dishes prepared in the frying pan.

## POTATOES IN THEIR JACKETS

Take potatoes cooked in their jackets.* Do not skin them. Drop them into a saucepan of boiling water. Let them heat for five to six minutes according to their size.

Serve them beneath a napkin with curls of fresh butter.

* I advise you to always have some of them in store.

## SAUTE POTATOES

Take some cold cooked potatoes. Skin them and cut them in slices a quarter of an inch thick.

Heat a piece of butter and a tablespoonful of oil ~~~~~~~~

~~~~~~~~ them as above. Mix the potatoes in a salad bowl with some oil, vinegar, a teaspoonful of cold water, salt, pepper and if possible some chopped tarragon.

## POTATOES WITH BACON

Cut some cooked potatoes in thin slices. Heat a small piece of butter smoking hot in a frying pan and then melt two ounces of fat bacon in small cubes.

Fry the potatoes in this fat and salt sparingly.

## POTATOES EN RAGOUT

Take some cooked potatoes. Peel them and cut them in slices about three-quarters of an inch thick.

Melt some butter in a frying pan and add a finely chopped onion. Let it turn golden brown. Add a dessertspoonful of flour. Brown it. Add, little by little, some cold water. Let it thicken, boil

Salt, pepper. Add half a bay leaf and your potatoes. Heat them for five minutes.

## POTATOES IN BECHAMEL SAUCE

Cut some cooked potatoes in thin slices. Prepare a Béchamel sauce. Mix it with the potatoes. Warm carefully as it is apt to stick.

By adding gruyère cheese to your sauce you can make Mornay potatoes.

## FRIED POTATOES

Put the deep frying pan on the gas. Peel some raw potatoes and cut them in wafer-thin slices.

When the fat is smoking put in the potatoes. Leave them five minutes. Take them out. Heat the fat until it smokes abundantly. Put in the potatoes once more. Leave them two minutes. Take them out. Sprinkle them with fine salt.

## PEAS

Buy cooked peas in a tin. A half pound tin is sufficient for two or three people. Open the tin. Pour the contents into a bowl. Drain off the liquid. There is always too much.

## GREEN PEAS WITH BUTTER

Melt some butter in a small saucepan. Add the peas and then two tablespoonfuls of juice from the tin.

Heat them for five minutes until they are almost boiling. If you think there is not enough water add some, but avoid serving the peas swimming in liquid like a soup.

## GREEN PEAS WITH BACON

in long thin strips. Warm up

### GREEN PEAS WITH CREAM

Prepare a small tin of peas with butter. While they are warming on the gas mix three ounces of thick cream in a bowl with half a teaspoon of flour. Mix the cream and the peas. Heat. Let them come to the boil once. If the sauce is too thick add a little of the juice from the tin. Salt to your taste. Do not pepper.

### BEANS

Buy tinned beans. They are already cooked and only need warming up.

### BEANS MAITRE D'HOTEL

Open a small tin of beans and pour them with their juice into a saucepan. Heat until they boil. Let them boil five minutes. Drain them into a colander. Put the beans back into the saucepan and on to the fire. Add two ounces of butter. Stir in delicately so as not to crush the beans. When the butter has melted add some chopped parsley. Salt as you wish and serve.

### BEANS IN CREAM

Prepare a small tin of beans *à la maître d'hôtel*. Before serving add three ounces of thick cream. Mix. Warm up. This is a most attractive dish.

### FRIED BEANS

Open a small tin of beans. Drain them in a colander.

Heat some butter smoking hot in a frying pan and add the beans. They begin to fry in the butter. Turn them over. Salt. Pepper lightly. Serve.

BEAN SALAD

## HARICOT BEANS BRETONNE

Melt two ounces of butter in a saucepan. Add a small tin of haricot beans, draining off all but two to three spoonfuls of their juice.

Warm them for five minutes. Add, if necessary, some water from the tin. Salt. Garnish with chopped parsley.

## FRIED HARICOT BEANS

Heat two ounces of butter to smoking point in a frying pan. Fry them golden brown. They are ready.

## HARICOT BEANS BASQUE

Warm two spoonfuls of olive oil in a frying pan. Add half a clove of garlic minced finely. When the garlic begins to colour add a small tin of haricot beans. Mix. Moisten slightly. Salt. Pepper copiously.

## FLAGEOLETS A LA CREME

Melt a piece of butter the size of a large walnut in a saucepan. Add a small tin of flageolets and three spoonfuls of their juice.

Mix two ounces of thick cream with half a teaspoonful of flour in a bowl. Mix the flageolets and the cream. Bring to the boil. Serve with a little chopped parsley.

## SAUERKRAUT

Buy some sauerkraut ready cooked as you will never have the time to do it yourself.

If you go to a good shop it will be far better than any you could prepare.

## SAUERKRAUT ALSACIENNE

Warm the sauerkraut in a saucepan adding a tablespoonful of white wine. In the meantime boil some Frankfurter sausages for five minutes.

Serve the sauerkraut, sausages and a slice of ham.

## SAUERKRAUT WITH
## CHIPOLATA SAUSAGES

Warm the sauerkraut. Fry some chipolata sausages in another pan. Serve.

## RAW SAUERKRAUT SALAD

Buy half a pound of raw sauerkraut. Wash it three times under running water so that most of the sourness is removed. Squeeze it dry in a napkin.

Season it with oil and salt.

This is a delicious accompaniment to fried sausages.

ARTICHOKES

Buy tinned artichoke h...

ASPARAGUS IN OIL

Serve this tinned asparagus cold with oil and vinegar, salt and pepper.

ASPARAGUS WITH HOLLANDAISE SAUCE

Warm the asparagus in a saucepan in its own juice. While it is warming prepare a *sauce hollandaise*. Serve together.

PUMPKIN

Buy a pound of pumpkin. Cut off the peel generously, without trying to be economical.

Cut the pulp into half-inch cubes.

Melt some butter in a frying pan; fry these cubes which soon become soft.

Serve well salted and peppered.

Or else, .instead of salt, sugar it. Then, of course, you serve it at the end of the meal.

## BEETROOT

Beetroot can be a very pleasant vegetable. Its possibilities are exploited far too little. Buy beetroot ready cooked as you would for making salad. Peel it, wash it, and you have your basis for making a number of dishes.

## MINCED BEETROOT A LA CREME

Peel and wash half a pound of beetroot cooked in the oven. Dry it. Chop it finely. Heat some butter in a frying pan until it smokes. Warm the beetroot in it. Salt. Add a teaspoonful of vinegar. The beetroot immediately turns to a flaming hue. Add two ounces of thick cream. Mix. Warm for two minutes. Serve with vinegar and salt. Arrange it in a small dish. Cover it with a blanket of thick cream. Serve as *hors d'œuvre*.

## BEETROOT WITH OIL AND VINEGAR

Slice some cooked beetroot. Season with oil, vinegar, salt, pepper and chopped fine herbs.

An excellent accompaniment to boiled beef.

## BEETROOT WITH HORSERADISH

Prepare a salad as above. Add some grated horseradish. Mix.

## CUCUMBERS

You can really only prepare these as salad.

## CUCUMBER SALAD

Peel a cucumber. Cut it in two lengthwise. Scoop out the seeds with a teaspoon. Cut the pulp into the finest possible strips. Sprinkle with fine salt. Arrange it in a salad bowl. Cover it with

Prepare the cucumbers as above. Season with salt, a very little vinegar and thick cream.

## TOMATOES

Tomatoes can be prepared very rapidly. In hot weather they are an invaluable stand-by.

## TOMATO SALAD

Slice some really ripe tomatoes. Season them with oil, vinegar, salt, pepper and fine herbs. In the South of France a clove of finely minced garlic is always added. In a temperate climate, however, this is not to be recommended.

## TOMATOES PROVENCALES

Cut two tomatoes in half horizontally.

Warm some oil in a frying pan. Add two shallots and an onion chopped small. Put the tomatoes in the frying pan face downwards. Leave them five minutes on a good fire. Turn them over. Using a fork, prick the skin in several places.

Cook on a hot fire for five minutes more. Salt. Pepper. Sprinkle with chopped parsley. Serve.

## TOMATOES A LA POLONAISE

Cut the tomatoes in two. Melt some butter in a frying pan. Add an onion finely minced. Put the tomatoes face downwards in the pan. Cook on a hot fire for five minutes. Turn. Pierce the skin with a fork. Cook for five minutes. Salt, pepper. Pour three ounces of thick cream between the tomatoes. Heat. Let the creamy sauce come to the boil. Serve.

## SPINACH

You can buy spinach in tins. Open it. Drain it in a colander. Do not use an iron pan to warm it or the spinach will turn black.

## SPINACH IN BUTTER

Melt some butter in a saucepan. Add the spinach. Heat. Mix. Salt. When the spinach is hot serve it with veal, eggs or even fish.

## SPINACH A LA CREME

As above. Finish by adding some thick cream. Mix. Heat. Serve.

## SORREL

Sorrel turns into a thick paste as soon as it comes into contact with heat. It is seldom used, yet it is the classic accompaniment to veal or certain fish.

## SORREL WITH GRAVY

Wash the sorrel. Melt a piece of butter in a saucepan. Add the sorrel. Heat. Stir with a wooden spoon. In five minutes the sorrel has turned brownish and has transformed itself into

cleaned. What is more, they do not contain much water. They can be rapidly cooked as this water does not take long to evaporate.

As for *cèpes,* you can buy them in tins. They can be used to provide a classic dish: *cèpes à la bordelaise.*

Mushrooms serve as an accompaniment to white meat, eggs and fish. Use them to excess in your rapid cookery. They bring about a happy transformation in every dish to which they are added.

## MUSHROOMS A LA CREME

Buy half a pound of forced mushrooms. Cut off the sandy base of the stem. Wash them in plenty of water. Lift them out of the basin. Throw away the water and sand. Repeat three times. Do not peel the mushrooms; cut them in slices. Wash them once more. Dry them in a cloth. Melt one ounce

**93**

of butter in a large saucepan. Add an onion finely minced; then the mushrooms. Cover. Make a hot fire. The water in the mushrooms evaporates. They boil. Lift off the lit. Let them boil hard in order to facilitate the evaporation. Salt. Pepper. At the end of six minutes a little liquid will remain; add two ounces of thick cream which you have mixed with half a teaspoonful of flour. Mix. The sauce is thickened. Serve. This is divine.

## CEPES BORDELAISE

Heat some olive oil in a frying pan. Add three shallots and a clove of garlic minced. Wash the *cèpes,* which you have taken out of the tin, in cold water. Put them into the frying pan. Heat them for six to seven minutes. Salt. Pepper. Sprinkle with finely-chopped parsley. Serve.

## FRIED MUSHROOMS

Place the deep frying pan containing lard on the gas.

Take half a pound of middle-sized mushrooms. Cut off the sandy base of the stem. Wash them very carefully as above and dry them in a cloth.

Dip the mushrooms in batter composed of a beaten egg, three spoonfuls of flour and enough beer to make a cream which is fluid but thick enough to coat the mushrooms.

Dip the mushrooms in this paste, and throw them one by one into the smoking fat. Fry for five to six minutes. Lift them out. Drain. Salt. It is delicious.

# VEGETABLE FLOUR

There are vegetable flours on the market which have already been cooked by means of

I recommend green pea flour, which makes excellent purées.

The method of preparation is the same for all kinds of vegetable flour.

Put two large spoonfuls of flour for each person into a small saucepan.

Mix with cold water until you have a thick paste which is just fluid enough to pour. See that you do not add too much water or the purée will be too liquid.

Put it on the gas. Salt and stir quickly while the purée thickens. At a certain moment it puffs up and bursts like a volcano. Turn down the gas, add some butter and let it melt. Wait for three to four minutes. The purée is ready. Taste, salt as you wish and add a little hot water if you find the purée too thick. But whatever happens, not too much. If there is too much water the purée takes on a disagreeable flavour.

## PUREE OF GREEN PEAS

Prepare a purée with green pea flour. Add some butter. Serve it with small forcemeat balls. This is a classic.

Instead of butter you can use fried diced bacon with its fat.

## LENTIL PUREE

The same technique as above, using lentil flour. A very good accompaniment to fried chipolata or Paris sausages. Pour the fat from the sausages over the purée.

## PUREE OF HARICOT BEANS

The technique as for green pea purée. Very good accompaniment to pork cutlets.

## CHESTNUT PUREE

Use very little water when you prepare the purée. Add water afterwards if it is necessary. Add butter, plenty of salt and a little pepper.

purée.

# SOME DELICATE, IF HASTY, DISHES

Beef is excellently suited to Express-cookery, since it is delicious when it is served underdone.

We will take it that all our dishes are for two people.

## ENTRECOTE WITH FRIED POTATOES

Heat the deep frying pan to smoking point on one of your fires, and prepare some fried potatoes. While they are crisping heat a tiny piece of butter in a frying pan on the other fire. When this is smoking, put in a fillet steak weighing ten ounces. Wait three minutes. Turn it. Wait three minutes more. Salt. Put it on a hot dish. Sprinkle with chopped parsley. Slip a piece of butter between the meat and the dish. Serve with the fried potatoes.

## ENTRECOTE WITH ONIONS

Do as above but when you lay the steak in the pan surround it with an onion finely sliced. The onion browns on the hot fire. Serve the steak covered with the fried onions.

## MINUTE STEAK

While the steak is frying in the pan cook half a pound of finely-sliced mushrooms and a minced shallot in butter in another pan. Make a blazing fire so that th...

Prepare an entrecôte steak on one fire. On the other make a *sauce béarnaise* with one yolk of egg and two and a half ounces of butter. This is quite sufficient. Serve the steak coated with the sauce.

## CHATEAUBRIAND WITH POTATOES

On one fire fry some sliced cooked potatoes in butter.

On the second fire heat some butter in another pan until it smokes. Put in a slice of fillet steak weighing about half a pound. Let it cook over a hot fire for three minutes. Turn the meat. Leave it three minutes on a fierce flame. Salt.

Put the châteaubriand on a hot dish. Surround it with sauté potatoes. Now enjoy yourself.

## TOURNEDOS WITH MADEIRA

Put two *tournedos* into a very hot buttered frying pan. Let them cook three minutes on each side. Put them on to a hot dish. Pour two table-spoonfuls of Madeira into the pan. Let it boil. Pour it on to the steak.


## TOURNEDOS DAUPHINOISE

Prepare half a pound of mushrooms à la crème in a frying pan.

In a second frying pan prepare two tournedos with Madeira.

Pour the mushrooms into a deep dish with the *tournedos* on top. Pour over them the Madeira sauce from the pan.


## TOURNEDOS ROSSINI

Prepare some *tournedos* with Madeira. Add some truffle peelings to the sauce.

Put the *tournedos* on to a very hot dish. Put a slice of truffled foie gras trimmed to the size of the meat on each *tournedos*. Pour the Madeira and truffle sauce over them.

This is a dish for special occasions.


## A GOOD BEEFSTEAK

Sometimes one must be satisfied with a simple beefsteak.

Buy ten ounces of rump steak. Make some butter smoking hot in a frying pan. Cook the steak three minutes on each side; salt, parsley and fried potatoes.

## RUSSIAN BITOCKS

Buy half a pound of minced beef. Mix this with a quarter of

egg and stir it in. Make four rissoles. Fry them in butter, four minutes on each side. Dissolve the glace in the pan

with a little wine and very little cognac. Pour this sauce over the *bitocks*. Serve with noodles which have been cooked in boiling water and tossed in fresh butter.

## VEAL

There will, of course, never be any question of joints of veal roasted slowly in the oven or cunningly concocted stews. We shall be confined to escalopes and cutlets. But these two will give us abundant satisfaction, as you will see.

## ESCALOPES OF VEAL

This is the simplest possible dish to prepare.

1. Put a little flour in a plate. Dip the two escalopes in the flour, seeing that they are well covered. Press the flour on to the meat with your finger tips. But only do this at the moment when you put the frying pan on the gas. The moisture in the meat must not penetrate the flour.

2. Put a piece of butter into the hot frying pan. Let it melt and then smoke. Lay in the escalopes; let them cook for two minutes. Turn them. Let them brown for two minutes. Turn them again and let them cook three minutes more.

This is not just a meaningless rite. It is necessary in order that the upper surface, covered with uncooked flour, may not be moistened by the juice from the meat. If this happened, the layer of damp flour would detach itself when you turned the escalope and the meat would not brown properly.

When the escalopes are golden brown, salt them. Lift them out of the pan and put them on to a hot dish. Pour a little water into the frying pan and let it boil. The water dissolves the caramel which has formed and you thus obtain a brown gravy, which you pour over the escalopes.

Serve them with noodles à l'anglaise which you have prepared on the second hotplate on your stove.

## ESCALOPES OF VEAL WITH OLIVES

Prepare one or two fried escalopes. First stone some green olives. Put them into the pan during the last three minutes of cooking. Take out the escalopes; leave the olives. Pour two spoonful of

Prepare two fried escalopes. Add a spoonful of tomato purée to the sauce. Mix the juice with the tomato. Heat for a minute and pour this flame-coloured sauce over the escalopes.

## ESCALOPES OF VEAL A L'ESPAGNOLE

Prepare two escalopes of veal with tomato sauce, but add some stoned black olives with the tomato. Warm the sauce and pour it over the escalopes.

## ESCALOPES OF VEAL MAGYAR

Prepare two fried escalopes. Add some paprika to the brown sauce. Serve with dumplings which you have prepared on the second hotplate.

## ESCALOPES OF VEAL BORDELAISE

Fry some escalopes of veal. In a second frying pan prepare some mushrooms *à la bordelaise* with olive oil and shallots.

Serve the escalopes surrounded by the mushrooms.

## ESCALOPES OF VEAL A LA CREME

Prepare some fried escalopes. Once the escalopes are on the dish and the brown sauce made in the frying pan add a tablespoonful of good thick cream. Mix it with the sauce; bring to the boil. Pour it over the escalopes.

Serve with some tinned green peas warmed and buttered on the second fire.

## ESCALOPES OF VEAL WITH CAPERS

Prepare some fried escalopes. When you make the sauce add a teaspoonful of capers. Heat through and pour it over the escalopes.

## ESCALOPES OF VEAL ZINGARA

Prepare some fried escalopes. In another pan fry some mushrooms in butter adding some ham coarsely chopped and some truffle peelings. When this is thoroughly hot add it to the gravy from the escalopes. Warm through and pour it over the meat. Eat with enjoyment.

## ESCALOPES OF VEAL VIENNOISE

Put the deep frying pan containing oil or lard on the gas. (Beef dripping should only be used for frying potatoes.)

Have three plates before you containing flour, beaten egg and white, or very light breadcrumbs.

Take the thinnest possible escalopes. Get the butcher to beat them as thin as possible. Make a series of little cuts round the edge.

Dip them into flour, egg and breadcrumbs. Throw them into the smoking fat. Wait until they are well browned—about six minutes. Lift them out, salt them and put them on to a hot dish. Decorate them with slices of lemon.

## FRIED VEAL CUTLETS

Treat them the same as fried escalopes. You can, however, omit the flour.

Brown them on both sides in butter. Dissolve the *glace* in the frying pan with some white wine. Pour it over the cutlets.

All the different combinations which I have mentioned for escalopes can be used for cutlets.

## VEAL CUTLETS MILANAISE

Prepare some veal cutlets in the same way as *escalopes viennoise*, that is to say, dip them in flour, egg and breadcrumbs.

Fry them in smoking butter. Salt. Serve pouring over them the butter from the frying pan to which you have added some fresh butter, which quickly melts.

## CUTLETS POJARSKI

These cutlets, which are *bitocks* of white meat, should really be made of chicken. Usually one uses veal.

Take six to eight ounces of minced veal. Mix four parts of this with one part of stale breadcrumbs, which have been soaked in milk and carefully squeezed to eliminate surplus moisture.

Mix the meat and bread with your finger tips. Salt, pepper and stir in the yolk of an egg. Make small flat cakes of the mixture and dip them in flour, yolk of egg and breadcrumbs. Fry them for eight to ten minutes in very hot butter.

Serve with green peas in butter prepared on the second fire.

# MUTTON

Mutton, which is delicious when it is under-done, is excellently suited to rapid cookery. Only

When the grill is very hot, that is to say, after it has been heating for five minutes, put the meat beneath it. Turn it after three minutes. Cook for three minutes more. Salt. Serve with fried potatoes which you have prepared in the meantime.

## FRIED CUTLETS
Fry some cutlets in the same way as steak—that is to say, three minutes on each side. Salt. Serve too with fried potatoes.

## ESCALOPES OF MUTTON
Buy some slices of mutton cut from the top of the leg or the saddle. Grill them or fry them and serve with fried potatoes.

## MUTTON CHOPS
Treat them in the same way as cutlets or escalopes, though they should be cooked two or three minutes longer.

## ESCALOPES OF MUTTON IN EGG AND BREADCRUMBS

Buy some slices of mutton. Dip them in flour, egg and breadcrumbs. Cook them in butter in a frying pan. Serve them with French mustard.

## SAUTE MUTTON A L'AMERICAINE

Buy two slices of mutton. Cut each in four pieces.

Dice two ounces of bacon. Warm the bacon in a frying pan with some butter. Add the mutton slices. Fry them from six to seven minutes in the bacon fat, and salt with restraint. Serve as they are on a hot dish.

## MUTTON A LA GEORGIENNE

Buy two slices of mutton. Cut each in four. Fry the pieces in butter. Salt. Pepper. Sprinkle with vinegar. Let it evaporate. Serve garnished with slices of raw onion. This dish should be eaten with one's fingers.

# PORK

Cutlets, grills, trotters in egg and breadcrumbs, ears, cheek, tail—such are the delights offered by this noble animal

put in the two cutlets and make a blazing fire. The fat melts, and mingles with the butter; the meat soon begins to brown.

Five minutes on one side, five minutes on the other and your cutlets are done to a turn.

Salt and serve with mustard. It is the simplest kind of preparation and quite sufficient, as the fat in the pan serves as sauce for the meat.

## PORK CUTLETS WITH APPLES

Peel some good Canadian apples and remove the core and pips. Cut them in small dice. Put them into a saucepan with very little water. Put them on the gas. Cover. Bring to the boil. After five minutes crush the softened pulp with a spoon. In ten minutes, if the apples are of good quality, the purée is ready. Salt, pepper.

While they are cooking prepare two cutlets of pork in the frying pan. Put them on a dish.

Surround them with apple purée. Pour the fat from the pan over the latter. Eat with mustard.

## PORK CUTLETS WITH ONIONS

Cut a large onion in small pieces. Put two pork cutlets into a pan containing very hot butter. Two minutes later arrange the chopped onion round the meat. Cook as usual, mixing from time to time the onions with the fat from the cutlets. Salt. Serve with mustard.

## CUTLETS OF PORK WITH NOODLES

Cook some noodles in boiling water. They are ready in ten minutes.

During this time prepare some fried cutlets of pork. Drain the noodles. Prepare them *à l'anglaise*. Put the cutlets on a dish. Surround them with noodles. Pour the fat from the pan over them.

## PORK CUTLETS WITH POTATOES

Take some cooked potatoes. Peel them and cut them in slices. Fry them in a pan containing a little lard.

In the meantime fry two pork cutlets. At the last moment put the sauté potatoes into the fat from the cutlets. Serve all together.

## PORK CUTLETS A L'ITALIENNE

Cook some noodles and prepare them *à l'anglaise*. While they are cooking fry some pork cutlets.

Take out the cutlets and add a good teaspoonful of purée to the fat and enough water to liquefy
the sauce.

Put the cutlets on a dish and cover them with
tomato sauce. Surround them with b...

Serve the cutlets surrounded with chestnut
purée, pouring the fat from the pan over both.

## PORK CUTLETS WITH HARICOT BEANS

Fry two pork cutlets. When half cooked surround them with cooked haricot beans. Mix the
beans and the juice. Serve all together.

## PORK CUTLETS WITH SAUERKRAUT

On one fire heat some ready-prepared sauerkraut. On the other fry some pork cutlets.

Serve the cutlets surrounded with sauerkraut
on which you pour the fat from the pan.

## GRILLED PORK

Buy some very thin slices of boned pork. These
rapidly crispen in smoking butter or lard. Salt,
pepper, serve with mustard.

## PIG'S TROTTERS IN EGG AND BREADCRUMBS

Certain shops sell pig's trotters ready egg and breadcrumbed.

One can brown them in a frying pan in smoking butter or lard. This is dangerous. The crust nearly always explodes. The explosion scatters fat.

It is better to dip them in frying oil and put them under the grill. One is no longer afraid of the spluttering fat.

It takes ten minutes to warm up these trotters. Serve them with mustard. This is an admirable dish but difficult to eat if one is anxious to leave no meat on the bone. One dirties one's fingers as much as one's mouth. But it is worth it.


## PIG'S EARS IN EGG AND BREADCRUMBS

The same treatment as for pig's trotters. Oil and grill. Mustard.


## PIG'S TAIL IN EGG AND BREADCRUMBS

Prepare like the ears and trotters. Unfortunately, these are very rarely to be had. It is true that each pig has only one tail for every pair of ears and eight half-feet. Perhaps this is the explanation.

# SAUSAGES AND SO ON

In many shops you will find materials for a

accompany them with a salad, follow them with
cheese and fruit, and you will have had a most
enviable meal.

There are other products which you must cook
or re-cook yourself and these are an invaluable
resource.

## SAUTE HAM

Put a slice of ham into a saucepan where some
butter is smoking. Cook it for two minutes on each
side. Serve it with sauté potatoes or green peas prepared in butter on your second fire.

## SAUSAGES

Heat some butter in a frying pan. Put in the
sausages which you have pierced here and there
with a fine skewer. The fire should be moderate.
Let them brown on one side for five minutes. Turn
them. Cook five minutes more. Put them on to a

hot dish. Heat some ready-cooked flageolets or haricot beans in the fat.

Serve together. It is delicious.

Sausages go very well with green pea purée.

## CHIPOLATA SAUSAGES

Fry as above. Serve with browned haricot beans or sauerkraut warmed up.

They are excellent, too, with fried eggs or tomato sauce.

## FRANKFURTER SAUSAGE

You buy these sausages in pairs.

Put them on the gas in a pan full of cold water. As soon as you see the slightest signs of boiling lower the gas and leave the sausages in their bath for ten minutes, on the fire, at a temperature of about 190°. If you let them boil they will probably burst.

Lift the sausages out of the water and serve them with potato salad or hot sauerkraut. The first combination is the more classic.

To eat the sausages hold them in your finger tips and bite into them. Above all, never prick them with a fork. The juice runs out and all is lost.

GRILLED CERVELAT SAUSAGE

Take two cervelats, strip off the skin. This is easy if you make an incision with a sharp knife.

Cut each sausage in two lengthwise. Put them

FRIED BLACK PUDDING

Buy really good black pudding. Cut it in pieces four to five inches long. On either side of each piece make three cuts with a very sharp knife. Fry the slices in hot butter on a very quick fire.

Serve with sauté potatoes or with a purée of Canadian apples which you have prepared according to the directions in the recipe for " Pork Cutlets with Apples " in the preceding chapter.

You must always eat mustard with black pudding.

PETIT SALE*

In some shops you find petit salé ready cooked. You should buy this often. Half cover it with boiling water. Cover the saucepan, put it on the gas and

*Petit Salé is a kind of salt pork.

boil for six to seven minutes, just long enough to heat through.

Serve with. tinned haricot beans which you have warmed in a frying pan with butter.

## TRIPE, ETC.

This includes much which is as suitable for the man in a hurry as for the gourmet. One does not preclude the other, although it is said that the gourmet always eats slowly and reverently.

Life nowadays has transformed all rhythms, and one frequently meets gourmets who have to be satisfied with food which has been rapidly cooked and, to their regret, rapidly eaten. But they are none the less gourmets for that.

### TRIPES A LA MODE DE CAEN

In certain shops it is possible to buy *tripes à la mode de Caen* already prepared. This takes the form of a calf's foot jelly in which morsels of ox stomach are imprisoned. In France this ranks as one of the glories of culinary art.

A pound of tripe is an ample portion for two people.

Put this block of tripe into a small saucepan. Add a spoonful of water. Put it on the gas, stirring all the time so that the gelatine melts and does not stick to the bottom of the saucepan. As soon as it is all melted and the pieces of tripe are floating freely in the liquid, lower the flame, cover the saucepan and leave it to heat for ten minutes.

Serve in a very hot soup plate with mustard.

If you wish to improve this dish, which is already exquisite, add, as soon as the gelatine ...

... it into a small saucepan. Add a glass of salted water. Bring it to the boil. Cover, wait seven to eight minutes. Lift it out of the water and drain.

Serve with oil and vinegar sauce and mustard.

## CALF'S HEAD IN TOMATO SAUCE

Prepare a tomato sauce. Put the calf's head, cut into two or three pieces, into the saucepan where the tomato sauce is heating. Cover. Heat. Salt and season. Serve.

## CALF'S HEAD MADRILENE

Prepare some calf's head in tomato sauce. Replace the butter by olive oil. Add some capers. Warm it; season copiously. Serve very hot.

## CALF'S HEAD TORTUE

Prepare some calf's head in tomato sauce. Add a liqueur glassful of Madeira or port to the sauce and two ounces of stoned olives. While this is warming, fry four or five chipolata sausages. Mix the calf's head, sauce and sausages.

This dish has great *allure* and no one will believe that it has been prepared so rapidly.

## FRIED CALF'S HEAD

Buy some ready cooked calf's head. Cut it in slices. Dip them in flour, beaten egg and breadcrumbs.

Fry these slices in butter. Salt and dust with paprika.

## BRAINS WITH BLACK BUTTER

Buy one or two sheep's brains. They are ready cleaned. Ox brains are cheaper but require the most scrupulously careful toilet to remove the veins and small clots of blood.

Bring salted water to the boil with some herbs: bay leaf, spice, etc. Put in the brains, which have been washed in cold water. Let them boil ten minutes.

While they are boiling brown some butter in the frying pan. Let it cool a little. Add a few drops of vinegar. Salt. Lift the brains out of the water. Lay them on a napkin so as to dry them as much as possible. Then put them on a plate; pour over the black butter and sprinkle with breadcrumbs.

## SHEEP'S KIDNEYS BROCHETTE

Get the butcher to cut the kidneys open. At home thread them on to a skewer in such a way that they do not curl up when cooking.

Heat some butter to smoking point in a pan. Put in the kidneys. Brown them for four minutes on one side. Turn them. Cook four minutes. Salt. Serve sprinkled with a little chopped parsley. Fried potatoes are the classic accompaniment.

## OX KIDNEY BEARNAISE

Ox kidney is despised. This is an injustice. Buy ten ounces of ox kidney for two people. Cut it in slices three-quarters of an inch thick.

Cook it like beefsteak in butter in a frying pan. Eight minutes are enough. Salt. Pepper. During this time prepare a *sauce béarnaise* on the other burner of your stove.

Serve the slices of kidney covered with the sauce. It is delicious.

## CALF'S KIDNEY SAUTE

Buy seven ounces of calf's kidney for two people. It is very expensive, I warn you. Have it cut into pieces the size of a small nut. Clean four ounces of mushrooms. Cut them into slices without peeling them.

Heat some butter in a frying pan until it smokes. Put in the kidney. Cook for five minutes.

Add the mushrooms. Salt. Pepper. Make a blazing fire, so that the water from the mushrooms evaporates. Put on a hot dish and serve.

## CALF'S KIDNEY WITH PORT

Prepare some sauté kidney. At the moment when you add the mushrooms pour three dessert-spoonfuls of port into the pan. Serve when it is half evaporated.

## CALF'S KIDNEY FLAMBE

Prepare some sauté calf's kidney. When you add the mushrooms pour in a small glass of brandy. Set it on fire in the pan. Finish cooking in the same way as for sauté kidneys.

Serve as it is without accompaniment.

## CALF'S KIDNEY A LA CREME

Prepare the sauté kidneys. Before serving add three ounces of thick cream mixed with half a tea-spoonful of flour. Mix all together. Bring to the boil. Salt and pepper. This is divine.

## CALF'S KIDNEY WITH MUSTARD

If you want a more exciting dish, prepare calf's kidneys in cream, but mix the cream with a good teaspoonful of French mustard. Otherwise proceed as for the previous dish.

## CALF'S LIVER SAUTE

Calf's liver is ruinous, but it is good. Ox liver is less expensive, but there is no comparison between them. The one remains tender after cooking—the other becomes tough. The latter must, therefore, be cooked for a very short time. Choose whichever you please.

on a dish. Pour melted butter over them. Decorate them with a dusting of very finely-chopped parsley.

## SAUTE LIVER A LA CREME

Prepare two slices of sauté liver. Before serving add three ounces of thick cream, mixing it with the butter. Serve the liver covered with the butter. Serve the liver covered with the sauce. Do not add any parsley.

## FRIED CALF'S LIVER

For this dish you must use calf's liver. Dip the two slices 1. in flour, 2. in beaten egg, 3. in bread-crumbs. Cook them in butter in a frying pan a little less hot than for the preceding dishes.

Cook four minutes on each side. Garnish them only with a slice of lemon.

## CALF'S LIVER A L'AMERICAINE

Buy a thick slice of ox liver weighing thirteen ounces. Have it cut in pieces the size of a nut. Buy three ounces of bacon. Dice it.

Melt a piece of butter in the frying pan. Add the pieces of bacon. Let them fry. After five minutes add the pieces of liver. Let them brown for five minutes. Dust with paprika. Salt cautiously, as bacon is sometimes already very salt.

Serve without garnish or with small slices of Cheshire cheese.

## POULTRY

There is no question of cooking a chicken or even a pigeon when one has only ten minutes in which to prepare a dish. We shall only be able to buy a ready roasted chicken.

But this does not mean that you are obliged to eat the chicken cold with salt. One can warm it up and make all sorts of salmis, and other delightful variations.

## COLD CHICKEN WITH MAYONNAISE

Simply serve the roast chicken with mayonnaise. It is quickly done and very good.

## CHICKEN SAUTE WITH MUSHROOMS

Buy a small roast chicken. Divide it into eight pieces—the two legs, the two wings, two halves of the breast and the carcase cut into two.

Melt some butter in a deep fireproof dish. Take a small finely-chopped onion and two ounces of diced bacon. Make a hot fire. After two minutes add half a pound of finely-chopped mushrooms.

Put the eight pieces of chicken immediately into the dish. Add half a glass of white wine in which you have dissolved half a teaspoonful of liquid meat extract. Cover. Turn the gas full on. Wait seven to eight minutes. Taste, salt. Now it is ready. Serve in the fireproof dish or in a deep dish which you have warmed.

## CHICKEN A LA CREME

As above, fry some bacon and onion and half a pound of mushrooms in butter in a fireproof dish.

Add the chicken. Pour in half a glass of water into which you have stirred a teaspoonful of liquid meat extract.

Before serving add four ounces of thick cream which you have first mixed with half a teaspoonful of flour. Mix the sauce and the cream rapidly. Bring to the boil. Serve.

### CHICKEN MARENGO
Prepare a sauté chicken, then before adding white wine mix it with a good spoonful of thick tomato purée. Warm it through. It is ready.

### PAPRIKA CHICKEN
Prepare a chicken *à la crème,* adding a teaspoonful of paprika when you begin cooking.

### FOIE GRAS
You have no time to prepare *foie gras* yourself, so buy it ready made.

One can buy good truffled *foie gras* in little earthenware jars or by weight in slices.

Do not spoil *foie gras* by any kind of preparation. Eat it as it is or simply with a slice of lettuce.


## GAME

You will neither eat jugged hare nor salmi of snipe. But if you think carefully you will find a number of game dishes sufficient to vary your menus and lend atmosphere to your table.

## QUAILS EN COCOTTE

A quail is a little too large to cook in ten minutes. It needs at least a quarter of an hour. So if you wish to prepare it rapidly, buy it already

egg and breadcrumbs in turn. Cook it in butter in a frying pan like a Wiener Schnitzl. Salt. Serve, pouring over it the butter from the pan, to which a piece of butter has been added and rapidly melted.

## VENISON CUTLETS

Buy some venison cutlets ready prepared. Cook them in a frying pan like lamb cutlets.

Dissolve the glace in the pan with three spoonfuls of dry white wine and half a glass of cognac. Boil for three minutes. Pour this over the cutlets and serve with chestnut purée.

## HARE A LA CREME

Have some slices cut from the hare's back across the back bone, about three-quarters of an inch thick.

Fry two slices in smoking butter for ten minutes, like mutton chops. Salt, pepper lightly.

Put two spoonfuls of dry white wine into the pan. Let it boil two minutes. Add three ounces of thick cream mixed with a teaspoonful of flour. Mix. Let it come to the boil once.

Serve the slices of hare in a deep dish covered with the sauce and surround with minced beetroots, which have been heated in the pan with butter and a little vinegar.

# THE FEW SWEETS
# WHICH CAN BE PREPARED
# IN TEN MINUTES

One can, in case of necessity, prepare one or two cold sweets provided one has the time to let them cool. Nothing is simpler than to prepare a sweet in the morning on getting up, and to keep it chilled ready to be eaten at mid-day.

Some sweets which are eaten hot can, on the other hand, be prepared at the last minute.

Here are some ideas:

## BREAD FRITTERS

Dip some slices of stale bread, from which you have removed the crust, into sweetened milk and then into beaten egg. Fry them on both sides in butter. Four minutes for each side is ample.

Serve hot sprinkled with castor sugar or with jam.

## OMELETTE FLAMBE

Prepare an omelette. Put it on a dish and sprinkle it with sugar. Pour slightly-warmed kirsch, cognac or rum over it ; set it on fire and serve.

... ...... .. .... .... . ......... .. ......... ..... a frying pan. Grease it with a piece of butter in a twist of fine linen rag. Pour in some of the paste, using a ladle. By tipping the frying pan, cover it entirely with a thin layer of paste. Put it on the fire for five or six seconds. Shake the frying pan. The pancake is loosened. Turn it. Twenty seconds cooking. Take it out. Make a second pancake and then the other four. Roll the finished pancakes as they are made. When they are all ready melt a large piece of butter in the pan. Put in the six pancakes. They brown on one side. Turn them. They become golden brown on the other. Serve them sprinkled with castor sugar. This does not take more than ten minutes if you are an expert.

## PANCAKES FLAMBE

Do as described above. Then pour slightly warmed kirsch or cognac over the pancakes. Set on fire. Serve with or without jam.

## APPLE FRITTERS

1. Put the deep frying pan on the gas. 2. Peel one or two apples and cut them in slices. Before peeling them take out the cores. 3. Break an egg into a small bowl. Add four dessertspoonfuls of flour. Mix with a wire beater. Add beer gradually, stirring all the time until you have a thick cream which coats a slice of apple which you dip into it. Salt slightly and add half a small glass of kirsch. Mix. When the lard or oil is smoking hot dip the slices of apple into the batter and throw them into the hot fat. Three minutes frying are enough. Lift the fritters out of the fat, drain and sprinkle with sugar. They are ready.

## ACACIA FRITTERS

In early summer dip bunches of acacia flowers into batter. Fry them in lard; sprinkle with sugar.

## STRAWBERRY FRITTERS

Dip the strawberries one by one into batter. Fry them in lard. Sprinkle them with sugar.

## BANANA FRITTERS

Cut some bananas lengthwise into two. Dip them into batter. Fry them in lard. Drain, sprinkle with sugar.

132

## SAUTE BANANAS

Cut some bananas into two lengthwise. Fry them in butter for a few minutes. Lift them out and sprinkle them with sugar mixed with a little

macaroons.

## CREAM CHEESE WITH CINNAMON

Beat the cream cheese with some cream and a little milk. Sugar and add some powdered cinnamon. This is a delicious sweet and rapidly prepared. Serve with or without biscuits.

## CREAM CHEESE WITH JAM

Serve a beaten sugared cream cheese. Cover it with a layer of raspberry or strawberry jam.

## FRUIT SALAD

Cut some apples, pears, pineapple and bananas in cubes. According to the season add strawberries or pieces of orange. Sprinkle with sugar. Pour some white wine over it and flavour with a small glass of kirsch or brandy. For a change replace the white wine by maraschino.

## STRAWBERRIES AND CREAM

Remove the stalks from the strawberries and sugar them. Cover them with cream whipped with a little port or cognac.

## CHESTNUT CREAM

Prepare a sweetened chestnut purée. For this, mix chestnut flour and castor sugar—one spoonful of sugar to two of chestnut flour. Add, as well, a little vanilla sugar, or a few drops of vanilla extract. Add milk until you have a thickish cream. Put it on the gas, stirring all the time. The cream thickens and bubbles. If it is too thick, add a little milk. Be careful, though, that it is not too liquid. Cook for three minutes. Pour it into a a plate and let it get cold. At the moment of serving cover with a layer of cream cheese whipped and slightly sugared.

It is a dish which has great *allure* and which is made in less than ten minutes. It is the triumph of method.

# INDEX

Frying . . . . . . . 11
Grilling . . . . . . . 12
Roasting . . . . . . . 13
Cooking in a frying pan . . . . 13
Thickening with flour . . . . 14
Thickening with egg . . . . . 16

Some Advice and some Menus
Kitchen equipment . . . . . 18
Some menus for lunch . . . . 21
Some menus for dinner . . . . 25
Some advice regarding behaviour at table . 28

Hors D'œuvres without Variations . . . . . . 33

Ultra Rapid Soups          37
Bouillon . . . . . . . 38
Semolina soup . . . . . . 39

Potage au jambon   .   .   .   .   .   39
Greek soup   .   .   .   .   .   40
Potage velouté .   .   .   .   .   40
Potage velouté with tarragon   .   .   40
Bouillon with parmesan   .   .   .   40
Beetroot soup .   .   .   .   .   41
Crème de cèpes .   .   .   .   .   41
Onion soup   .   .   .   .   .   42
Sorrel soup   .   .   .   .   .   42
Tomato soup   .   .   .   .   .   42
Pumpkin soup .   .   .   .   .   43
Aïgo-boulido   .   .   .   .   .   43
Pea soup .   .   .   .   .   .   43
Potage Esau   .   .   .   .   .   44
Fish Soup   .   .   .   .   .   44

## Extemporary Sauces

White sauce   .   .   .   .   .   47
Sauce Normande   .   .   .   .   48
Sauce Suprême .   .   .   .   .   48
Sauce Aurore   .   .   .   .   48
Sauce Poulette .   .   .   .   48
Béchamel sauce   .   .   .   .   48
Sauce Mornay .   .   .   .   49
Curry sauce   .   .   .   .   .   49
Sauce Piquante   .   .   .   .   50
Mustard sauce .   .   .   .   50
Sauce Robert   .   .   .   .   50
Mayonnaise sauce   .   .   .   .   51

Sauce Hollandaise . . . . . 51
Sauce Béarnaise . . . . . 52
Tomato sauce . . . . . . 53

Œufs sur le plat . . . . . 59
Eggs and bacon . . . . . 59
Eggs and ham . . . . . . 59
Eggs with cervelat sausage . . . 59
Eggs with cream . . . . . 60
Scrambled eggs . . . . . 60
Omelette . . . . . . 61

Some of the very few kind of
"Pâte" which can be
prepared in less than ten
minutes

Nouilles à l'anglaise . . . . . 65
Nouilles à l'italienne . . . . 65
Nouilles à la tchèque . . . . 65
Nouilles à l'espagnole . . . . 65
Noodles with gravy . . . . . 65
Alsatian dumplings . . . . . 65
Ravioli . . . . . . . 66

## Fish which only ask to jump from the pan into your plate

Whiting . . . . . . . 68
Skate with black butter . . . . 68
Haddock . . . . . . . 70
Cod with tomato sauce . . . . 70
Halibut sauce Mornay . . . . 70
Fried herring . . . . . . 70
Fried mackerel . . . . . . 71
Fresh sardines . . . . . . 71
Truite meunière . . . . . 71
Boiled trout . . . . . . 72
Fillets of sole with mushrooms . . . 72
Plaice meunière . . . . . 73
Fried whitebait . . . . . 73
Fried whiting . . . . . . 73
Fillets of cod viennoise . . . . 74
Boiled cod . . . . . . 74
Creamed cod . . . . . . 74
Biscay cod . . . . . . 75
Fried cod . . . . . . . 75

## MOLLUSCS AND SHELLFISH

### Molluscs

Oysters and sausages . . . . . 76
Snails . . . . . . . 76

Moules marinière . . . . . 77
Moules poulette . . . . . 78
Mussels with saffron . . . . . 78

Shellfish

Potatoes

Potatoes in their jackets . . . . 82
Sauté potatoes . . . . . . 83
Potato salad . . . . . . 83
Potatoes with bacon . . . . . 83
Potatoes en ragoût . . . . . 83
Potatoes in Béchamel sauce . . . 84
Fried potatoes . . . . . . 84

Peas

Green peas with butter . . . . 84
Green peas with bacon . . . . 85
Green peas with ham . . . . 85
Green peas with cream . . . . 86

Beans

Beans maître d'hôtel . . . . . 86
Beans in cream . . . . . . 86

Fried beans . . . . . . 86
Bean salad . . . . . . 87

Haricot Beans
Haricot beans bretonne . . . . 87
Fried haricot beans . . . . . 87
Haricot beans basque . . . . 87
Flageolets à la crème . . . . . 88

Sauerkraut
Sauerkraut alsacienne . . . . 88
Sauerkraut with chipolata sausages . . 88
Raw Sauerkraut salad . . . . 88

Artichokes . . . . . 89

Asparagus
Asparagus in oil . . . . . 89
Asparagus with hollandaise sauce . . 89

Pumpkin . . . . . . 89

Beetroot
Minced beetroot à la crème . . . 90
Beetroot with oil and vinegar . . . 90
Beetroot with horseradish . . . . 90

Cucumber
Cucumber salad . . . . . 91
Cucumber à la crème . . . . 91

T o m a t o e s
Tomato salad . . . . . . 91
Tomatoes provençale . . . . 91
Tomatoes à la polonaise . . . . 92

Mushrooms à la crème . . . . 93
Cèpes bordelaise . . . . . 94
Fried mushrooms . . . . . 94

V e g e t a b l e   F l o u r
Purée of green peas . . . . . 96
Lentil purée . . . . . . 96
Purée of haricot beans . . . . 96
Chestnut purée . . . . . 97
Purée of broad beans . . . . . 97

SOME DELICATE, IF HASTY, DISHES

B e e f
Entrecôte with fried potatoes . . . 100
Entrecôte with onions . . . . 100
Minute steak . . . . . . 101
Entrecôte béarnaise . . . . . 101

Châteaubriand with potatoes . . . 101
Tournedos with madeira . . . . 101
Tournedos dauphinoise . . . . 102
Tournedos Rossini . . . . . 102
A good beefsteak . . . . . 102
Russian bitocks . . . . . . 103

V e a l
Escalopes of veal . . . . . 104
Escalopes of veal with olives . . . 105
Escalopes of veal with tomatoes . . 105
Escalopes of veal à l'espagnole . . . 105
Escalopes of veal magyar . . . . 105
Escalopes of veal bordelaise . . . 105
Escalopes of veal à la crème . . . 106
Escalopes of veal with capers . . . 106
Escalopes of veal Zingara . . . . 106
Escalopes of veal viennoise . . . 106
Fried veal cutlets . . . . . 107
Veal cutlets milanaise . . . . 108
Cutlets Pojarski . . . . . 108

M u t t o n
Grilled cutlets . . . . . . 109
Fried cutlets . . . . . . 109
Escalopes of mutton . . . . . 109
Mutton chops . . . . . . 109
Escalopes of mutton in egg and bread-
    crumbs . . . . . . 110
Sauté mutton à l'americaine . . . 110
Mutton à la georgienne . . . . 110

Pork

Fried pork cutlets . . . . . 111
Pork cutlets with apples . . . . 111
Pork cutlets with onions . . . . 112
Pork cutlets with noodles . . . . 112

Pig's ears in egg and breadcrumbs . . 114
Pig's tails in egg and breadcrumbs . . 114


Sausages and so on

Sauté ham . . . . . . 115
Sausages . . . . . . . 115
Chipolata sausages . . . . . 116
Frankfurter sausages . . . . . 116
Grilled cervelat sausage . . . . 117
Fried black pudding . . . . . 117
Petit salé . . . . . . . 117


Tripe, etc.

Tripes à la mode de Caen . . . . 118
Calf's head in oil . . . . . 119
Calf's head in tomato sauce . . . 119
Calf's head madrilène . . . . 119
Calf's head tortue . . . . . 119
Fried calf's head . . . . . 120

Brains with black butter . . . . 120
Sheep's kidneys brochette . . . . 120
Sheep's kidneys grilled . . . . 121
Ox kidney bearnaise . . . . . 121
Calf's kidney sauté . . . . . 121
Calf's kidney with port . . . . 122
Calf's kidney flambé . . . . . 122
Calf's kidney à la crème . . . . 122
Calf's kidney with mustard . . . 122
Calf's liver sauté . . . . . 122
Sauté liver à la crème . . . . 123
Fried calf's liver . . . . . 123
Calf's liver à l'americaine . . . . 124

Poultry

Cold chicken with mayonnaise . . . 124
Chicken sauté with mushrooms . . . 124
Chicken à la crème . . . . . 125
Chicken Marengo . . . . . 126
Paprika chicken . . . . . 126
Foie gras . . . . . . 126

Game

Quails en cocotte . . . . . 127
Quail à la crapaudine . . . . 127
Venison cutlets . . . . . 127
Hare à la crème . . . . . 127

# THE FEW SWEETS WHICH CAN BE
## PREPARED IN TEN MINUTES

Bread fritters . . . . . . 130
Omelette flambée . . . . 130

Cream cheese and pineapple . . . 133
Cream cheese with cinnamon . . . 133
Cream cheese with jam . . . . 133
Fruit salad . . . . . . 133
Strawberries and cream . . . . 134
Chestnut cream . . . . . 134